For Lucy

Copyright © 1996 by Colin West

First U.S. edition 1996

Library of Congress Cataloging-in-Publication Data

West, Colin.
"Buzz, buzz, buzz," went Bumblebee / Colin West. — 1st U.S. ed.
Summary: Bumblebee buzzes around bothering everyone
until he comes to a gentle butterfly who understands that the
busy bee is looking for someone to be his friend.
ISBN 1-56402-681-7
[1. Bees — Fiction. 2. Butterflies — Fiction.
3. Friendship — Fiction.] I. Title.
PZ7.W51744Bu   1996
[E] — dc20   95-35204

10 9 8 7 6 5 4 3 2 1

Printed in Hong Kong

This book was typeset in Plantin.
The pictures were done in watercolor and ink.

Candlewick Press
2067 Massachusetts Avenue
Cambridge, Massachusetts 02140

"Buzz, Buzz, Buzz," went Bumblebee

COLIN WEST

CANDLEWICK PRESS
CAMBRIDGE, MASSACHUSETTS

.........as he landed on Butterfly's wing.........

Butterfly
said —

..."Buzz, buzz, buzz," went Butterfly............

.............and Bumblebee.....

.......and they buzzed away....

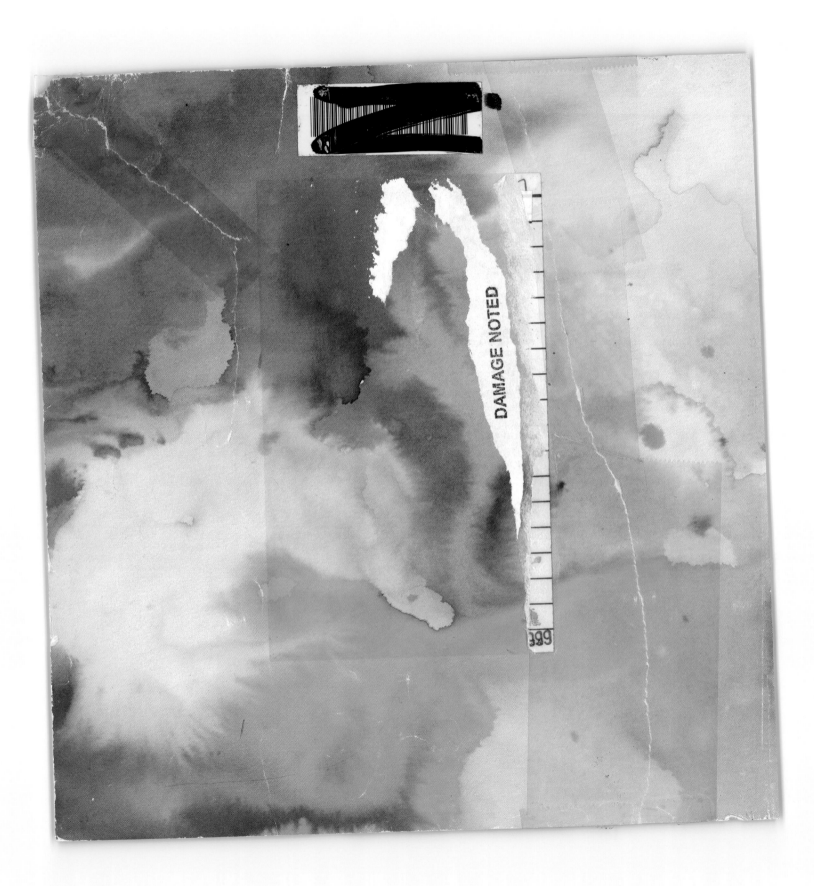

DAMAGE NOTED